The Berenstain Bears

BLAZE A TRAIL

Through deepest wood
and darkest trail —
Will the Bear Scout march
succeed or fail?

"This way, Scouts!"
Brother Bear said.
"Let's go while Papa
is still in bed!
Let's blaze a trail
through the wood
by ourselves—
the way Scouts should!"

But Papa was *not*
still in bed.
He was waiting for them
up ahead....
"This way, Scouts!
Let's blaze that trail!
With me along
you cannot fail!"

8

"Wait," said Brother,
"for Scout Leader Jane.
Look! Here she comes now
in her plane.
She's going to watch us
from the air!"
She wasn't too pleased
to see Papa Bear.

9

"What you Scouts need
is a guide like me!
I'll get you those badges!
Come! You'll see!

"This way, Scouts!
That way is wrong.
That twisty way
will take too long!"

"But, Papa! The guidebook says:
'When blazing a trail
through swamp or bog,
NEVER step on a sunken log!'"

YEEOOOOW!

"And that log," said Sister,
"is a crocodile!"
Pa blazed that trail
Papa Bear style!

"Wow!" said Fred.
"This is good!
A whole new trail
right through the wood!"

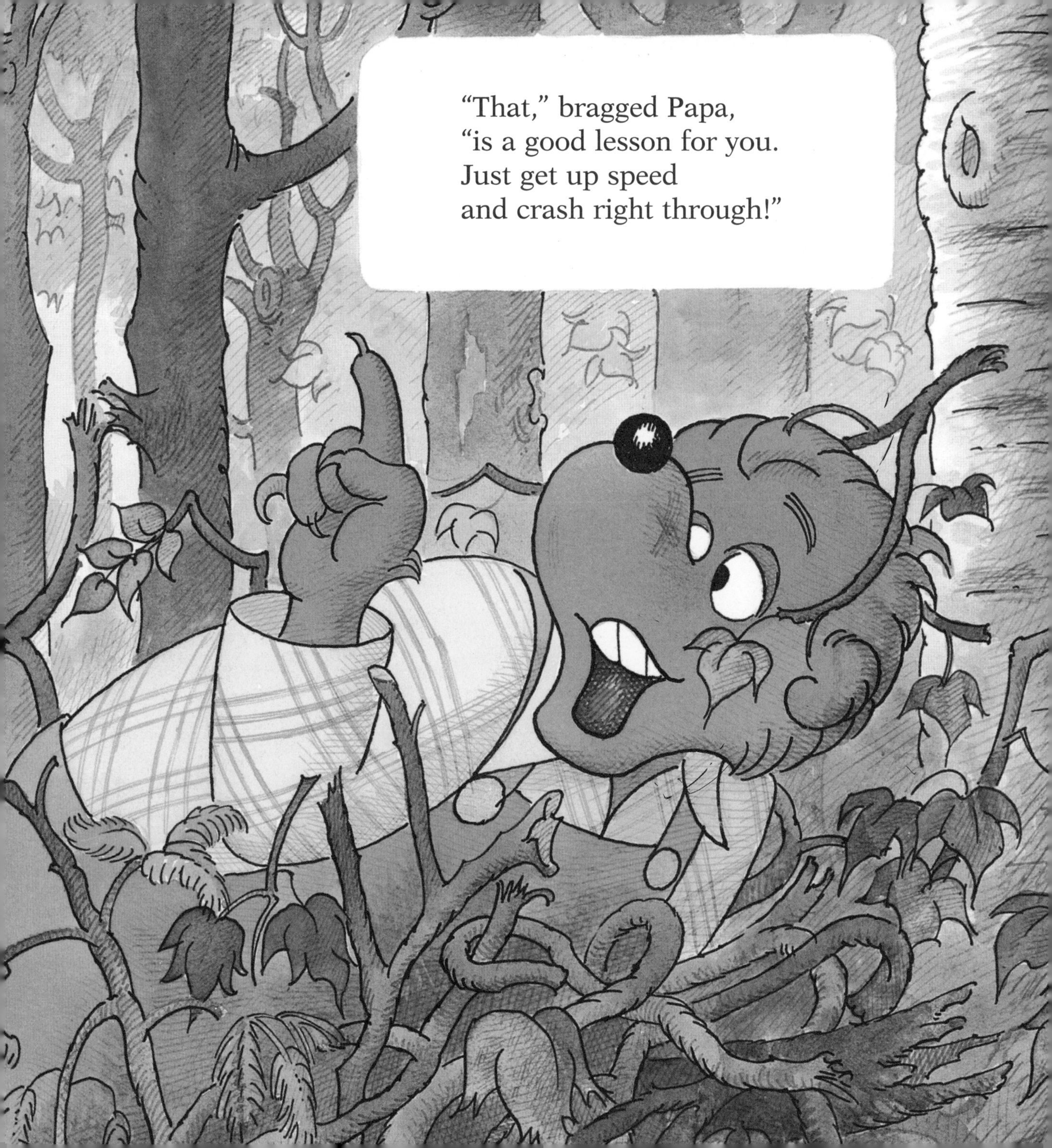

"That," bragged Papa,
"is a good lesson for you.
Just get up speed
and crash right through!"

"'Now, mark the trail,'"
Sister read from the book,
"'so others can follow
the path you took.'"

"Pooh!" said Papa.
"Twig signs are not for me.
Here! Watch this—
I use a tree!"

Then he went flying
through the air—
into a nest! An eagle's nest!

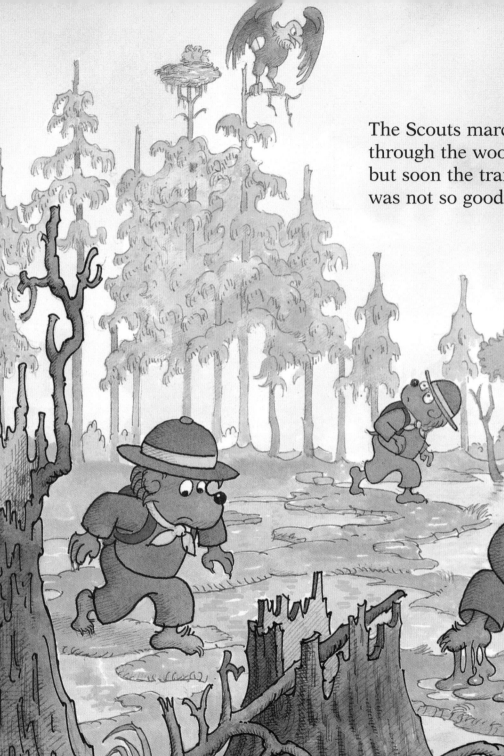

The Scouts marched on
through the wood,
but soon the trail
was not so good.

"This won't last,"
said Papa Bear.
"While I was up that tree
back there,
I could see
for miles around.
Come! This is the way
to higher ground!"

"This ground is good.
It's higher and drier.
Just the place
for our cooking fire."

"But, Pop," said Brother.
"We don't need to cook.
We have our trail rations.
Lots of them! Look!"

"Trail rations? Pooh!
I'll cook up a batch
of my delicious
trailblazer stew!"

"When on the trail,
wild things are best!
All cooked up
in an old bird's nest!"

"Now for a taste of my delicious trailblazer stew—

—PEW!"

25

"On second thought,
stew's not on my diet.
Er—about that trail food—
I think I'll try it!"

"Come!" shouted Papa.
"Your merit badges
are almost won!
Through Rocky Gorge,
and the test is done!"

"Shush, Papa! Shush!
It says in the guide:
'In rocky places do not shout—
a noise can cause rocks to slide!'"

But Sister's warning
came too late.
"Can't hear!" shouted Pa.
"The noise of these rocks
is much too great!"

Then Jane, who was watching
all the while,
landed her plane
on Pa's rock pile.

"Your merit badges!"
the scout leader said.
"For Brother . . . for Sister . . .
for Cousin Fred!
And one badge more . . . ,"
added Leader Jane.
"One for Papa!
I shall explain."

"Papa, you blazed a trail.
You did it fast.
Your three landmarks
are sure to last.

"First, we have Crocodile Alley,
thanks to you.

"Second, the smell
made by your stew.

"The third landmark
I have in mind
is the great rock pile
you left behind!"

"We did it, Scouts!
We knew we could.
We did what
we said we would.
We won badges
to wear with pride
by following
our *Bear Scout Guide*!"

The Berenstain Bears
and the
MISSING HONEY

There's no case too hard,
no case too tough,
for the Bear Detectives
and their hound dog, Snuff!

Papa's blackberry honey
was not in the jar!
Whoever took it
could not have gone far.
"We'll find it, Papa,"
Sister Bear said.
Then Brother Bear
whistled for Cousin Fred.

Cousin Fred came
with his sniffer hound, Snuff.
He also had
their detective stuff.

The Bear Detectives
looked all around.

Here are some of the clues
they found:

some fur,

some wax . . .

and a bit of cloth
that was red and yellow.

"Great!" said Papa.
"These clues will help us
find the fellow!"

"Ask Owl," said Mama.
"It's my belief
he might very well
have seen the thief."
"Tut, tut!" said Papa.
"What can he say?
Why, that sleepy old owl
sleeps all day!"

That's when Snuff
started sniffing the air.
"He's onto the scent!"
shouted Papa Q. Bear.

Snuff smelled blackberries
when he sniffed at the scent.
"Ruff!" said Snuff,
and away they all went.

"Be careful, now,"
said Papa Bear.
"That honey thief
could be anywhere!
Ah! The scent
is coming from
right over there!"

"Oh, no!" said Sister.
"Wait, Papa! Stop!
That is Beartown's
fanciest shop!"

But Papa and Snuff
burst into a room
where the fancy shop sold
BLACKBERRY PERFUME—

and many other kinds as well....
What a mess! What a smell!

"Excuse me, madam.
Sorry about that—
Come, cubs!" said Papa
as he tipped his hat.

"Our search for the thief
has just begun.
The honey thief
could be anyone.

"The butcher, the baker,
the candlestick maker.
Hmm! Yes, indeed—
the CANDLESTICK MAKER!"

"Bear Detectives,
you may relax.
The key to the crime
is our bit of wax!"

Then Papa and Snuff
dashed into that store—
right past a GONE FISHING
sign on the door.

The detectives were stumped.
But then on the breeze
came a scent so strong,
it made Snuff sneeze.

AH
CHOO!

"Look at that shirt!
It's red and yellow!
Just like the clue
from the robber fellow!"

"But, Papa," said Brother,
"that's not the shirt of a HE.
The clothes on that line
are the clothes of a SHE!"

"Son, it wouldn't matter
if it were my own mother.
A thief's a thief!"
said Papa to Brother.

Then the crook of a cane
came out from a wall.
It tripped Papa up.
It made Papa fall.

"I've something to tell you,
Papa," said Brother.
"This is Grizzly Gran's place!
She IS your own mother!"

Again no honey,
in spite of a clue!
Snuff had sniffed
Gran's blackberry stew!
So they headed home,
tired and sad—
the three Bear Detectives,
Snuff, and Dad.

But wait! Had Snuff once more
picked up a scent?
Up the front steps
of the tree house he went!

Up to the bedroom
where Ma and Pa slept.
Into the drawer
where Pa's things were kept.

"What is it?" cried Fred.
"What is it, old fellow?"
Snuff held up something
that was red and yellow!

"Hmm," said Fred.
"How strange. How funny.
This pajama top smells
like blackberry honey!"

"Here," said Brother,
"let me have a look—
the bit of cloth matches!"
Was Papa the crook?

"Clues do not lie,"
Sister Bear said.
"Look! The fur matches too!"
whispered Cousin Fred.

"Me, the thief? That's crazy!"
cried Pa with a howl.
That's when they heard
from sleepy old Owl.

"I saw the whole thing.
I can put everything right.
I saw Papa walk
in his sleep last night.

"He carried a candle
down to the shed,
drank up the honey,
and went back to bed!"

THE CLOTH

THE WAX

"I didn't dare wake him.
His sleep was so deep!"

"Then I wasn't the thief!
I walked in my sleep!"

"The case is solved!
No case is too tough
for the Bear Detectives
and our good sniffer, Snuff!"

The Berenstain Bears

and the PAPA'S DAY SURPRISE

Some papa bears are embarrassed by sentiment and pretend not to want a Father's Day present.

Papa Bear is a bear of many opinions. He has opinions about all sorts of things. He has an opinion about the best way to fell trees.

TIMBER-R-R!

He has an opinion about
predicting the weather.

THE BEST WAY TO PREDICT
THE WEATHER IS BY OBSERVING
THE LENGTH OF THE WOOLLY
BEAR CATERPILLAR'S COAT.

He has an opinion about
the best kind of honey.

NO QUESTION
ABOUT IT,
WILD, WILD HONEY
IS THE BEST!

And though in his opinion, Mother's Day is a fine and proper holiday and a worthy tribute to the institution of motherhood, he didn't think much of Father's Day.

LET'S JUST SKIP FATHER'S DAY THIS YEAR. IT'S JUST A SCHEME TO GET FOLKS DOWN TO THE MALL TO BUY LOTS OF GIFTS, NOT TO MENTION A BUNCH OF ICKY-STICKY FATHER'S DAY CARDS.

"That's fine with us," said Mama. "It's a busy time for me with the quilting bee coming up. And with the school year ending, the cubs are going to be pretty busy, too."

"Then it's agreed," said Papa. "We are not going to make a fuss about Father's Day."

A few days later, Papa was fixing a
creaky front step, Mama was working
on her tulip bed, and Baby Honey
Bear was playing on the grass. Above
their heads a pair of robins was hard
at work building a nest.

"The fuss about Father's Day is a lot of nonsense," said Papa. "Look at that daddy robin helping that mama robin build a nest. He doesn't need to have a fuss made over him. He's happy to do his job building the nest, sitting on the eggs when the time comes, and digging up worms when the chicks hatch. That daddy robin doesn't need a special day, and neither do I."

"Yes, dear," said Mama.

Papa was about to continue when he heard a noise in his shop. "Hey," he said, "there's somebody rooting around in my shop. If it's those pesky raccoons again, I'll…"

But it wasn't raccoons. It was Brother and Sister Bear.

"What are you two up to?" asked Papa.

"Er—we're just getting some stuff for a school project," said Brother.

"Er, that's right," said Sister, "a school project." Brother was holding a piece of the special paper that Papa used for his furniture designs. Sister was holding a roll of the paper Papa put down when he was painting.

"Okay," said Papa. "Just so it's got nothing to do with Father's Day. Is that clear?"

"Very clear," said the cubs.

But as Father's Day drew
closer, talk about it was very
much in the air—and *on* the air
as well:

on the radio,

AND NOW, WITH FATHER'S DAY APPROACHING, A WORD OF TRIBUTE TO ALL YOU DADS OUT THERE

on television,

at the mall,

and just about everywhere else.

Just as the drip, drip, drip of water can wear away solid rock, the constant talk about Father's Day began to wear away Papa's opinion about Father's Day.

75

A couple of days before Father's Day, Mama and Papa were in the living room. Mama was putting the finishing touches on a quilt.

"You know," said Papa, "I think maybe I'm being a little selfish about Father's Day. It's a lot of nonsense, of course. But cubs are cubs, and if they want to make a little fuss about it..."

"Sorry, dear," said Mama. "I was counting stitches and didn't hear a word you were saying."

Then the phone rang and Mama picked it up. "Yes," she said, "this is she. Yes, Mrs. Bruin. It's all arranged. See you there. Goodbye."

"What was *that* about?" asked Papa.

"Er—just some quilting business," said Mama.

"By the way," said Papa, "where *are* the cubs?"

"They're over at Cousin Fred's working on a big scout project," said Mama.

"Oh," said Papa. "I thought they were working on a big *school* project."

"Er—that's right," said Mama. "It's a big school *and* scout project."

Papa would never have admitted it, but he was beginning to hope that Mama and the cubs wouldn't worry about his opinion regarding Father's Day. He even looked in drawers and closets for hidden presents.

But there weren't any.

Now it was the day before Father's Day. Papa was on his way to his shop when he noticed the daddy robin. Mama robin had laid the eggs and the daddy was sitting on them.

"Mr. Robin," said Papa, "I think Mama and the cubs are up to something. And I think I know what it is: It's Father's Day! They're going to surprise me."

Mr. Robin didn't say anything. He just sat there.

Papa knew what Mama and the cubs were doing. They were *pretending* to skip Father's Day. Well, two could play at that game. Tomorrow morning, when he woke up to breakfast in bed and lots of presents and cards on Father's Day, he would pretend to be surprised.

But the next morning he didn't have to pretend. He really *was* surprised! There was no breakfast in bed! There were no gifts and cards!

But wait a minute! What was that delicious smell coming up from the kitchen? It was his favorite food: French-fried honeycomb. There *was* going to be a Father's Day breakfast. It just wasn't going to be in bed.

But the French-fried honeycomb wasn't for him at all. Mama explained that it was a gift for the new family down the road.

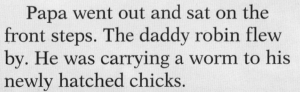

Papa went out and sat on the front steps. The daddy robin flew by. He was carrying a worm to his newly hatched chicks.

"Happy Father's Day, Mr. Robin," said Papa. "For all the good it's going to do us."

At that moment Mama and the cubs came down the front steps.

"Where are you going?" asked Papa. "What about breakfast?"

"We're all going for brunch at the Grizzmore Grille."

"Huh?" said Papa.

"The Grizzmore Grille, please," said the cubs as they piled into the car.

When they arrived, folks were lined up at the entrance.

"Look!" said Papa. "There's a sign over the door that says, 'Welcome, Dads'!"

"So there is!" said Mama with a big grin.

There was a much bigger sign inside. It said, *"Welcome to the Papa's Day Surprise."* It was painted on the roll of paper the cubs had gotten for the "school project." And there was a stage with a long table.

"Go ahead, Papa," said the cubs. "Up on the stage with the other papas."

He found a chair with his name on it at the long table. Other papas were on the stage with him: Lizzy Bruin's papa, Cousin Fred's papa, even Too-Tall's papa. Other papas filled the seats. And the food! All Papa's favorites: French-fried honeycomb, honey-cured salmon, honeyed squash.

Someone began to speak. It was Mayor Honeypot. "And now we shall hear from those who put this wonderful surprise together. Our first speakers will be Brother and Sister Bear."

Brother and Sister cleared their throats and read a poem. It was on the special paper they had taken from Papa's shop.

To the best Papa Bear
in the whole wide world:
You are big and strong and true.
And no matter what we do,
we know we can depend on you.
You cheer us on when we are glad.
You cheer us up when we are sad.
You are always there for us,
to help, advise, and care for us.
Happy Father's Day!

Papa looked out over the audience. But he could hardly see. His eyes were misty and he had a lump in his throat as big as a cantaloupe. After Brother and Sister read their poem, it was Lizzy Bruin's turn to say something about her dad. After Lizzy came Cousin Fred. As the cubs read their tributes, Papa thought about all the wonderful moments he had shared with his family. Well, they weren't always wonderful. But they certainly were moments.

Suddenly there was the sound of applause and cheering. It brought Papa back to the here and now of the Papa's Day Surprise. Cubs and mamas were on their feet. It had been a wonderful party and a wonderful Father's Day!

The guests headed for their homes.

"Cubs," said Papa as he drove down the hill to their tree-house home, "I want to thank you for that lovely poem."

"Mama helped us with it," said Brother.

"Also," said Papa, "I want to thank you for the Papa's Day Surprise. It was a wonderful gift."

"That," said Sister, "was a gift for *all* the papas. We and Mama have a special gift just for you."

"Just for me?" said Papa. He pulled to a stop at the tree house. He hurried up the front steps, through the front door, and into the living room.

When he saw what was waiting for
him, he could hardly believe his eyes.
"A Bearcalounger!" he cried.
"Just what I've always wanted!"
It was a special chair that
you could adjust up and
down. It was the perfect
chair for Papa.

Baby Honey began to
cry. She was hungry.

It was *also* the perfect place to feed Baby Honey. Mama and the cubs watched with big smiles as Papa sat back in his new Bearcalounger and gave Baby Honey her bottle.